THE
Family
FORTUNE

The Santini Family #3

S.L. SINCLAIR

Cover Design, Formatting by:

Partners in Crime Book Services

ISBN: 979-8-9988203-2-8

Table of Contents

Dedication

To all of my Sinners, who read The Family Firm *and thought, "Oh, I need more of this twisted shit!" It's because of you I have a career.*

Thank you.

Content Warning

<u>Please skip this page if you do not want a warning.</u>

This book is meant for readers above the age of 18 due to sexual content, dubious consent, non-consent, stalking, physical abuse, murder.
It also includes MM+ content and incest.
Read at your own discretion.

Also by S.L. Sinclair

Wife for Hire

Beyond Her Duties

The Family Firm

The Family Secret

The Family Fortune

Call Me Danger

Don't Get Me Twisted

Perfect Martinis

Unbiased

Acts of Contrition

Her Secret Master

Perfect Disaster

The Vampire Mistress

Lie To Me

Playlist

"Seven" by Jung Kook ft. Latto

"Symptom of Being Human" by Shinedown

"Let There Be Love" by Oasis

"Too Much" by The Kid Laroi, Jung Kook, Central Cee

"Cry For Help" by Shinedown

"Throw Me Away" by KoRn

"Instinct" by Dynazty

"Starving" by Hailee Steinfeld ft Zedd

"Unified" by Amaranthe

Chapter One

Sasha

Y PHONE SHOUTS "*DAMN!*" at me and I know it's the special notification I have for two things: my favorite singer goes live, or one of my fiancés texts me.

Since all three of my fiancés are home and asleep, I am going to assume it's the singer. I check my phone and, yep, he's live, talking about his new single. I set my phone up next to me on the coffee table and continue my work as I listen to him talk. It's Saturday morning, and I convinced my men we can work at home on Saturdays. It's usually only paperwork, and it doesn't matter where we are when we do it, right?

Plus, being home an extra day makes it easier to get them naked. Office sex is fun, but clothes usually have to stay on. Which is less fun. Sometimes.

"Morning, tesoro," Uncle Tony says as he enters the room. He pauses when he hears the voice. "You on video call?"

"No," I reply, gesturing to my phone. I'm sitting cross-legged in front of the coffee table, two empty cups of said coffee at my side. "Livestream."

"Ah, I'll leave you to it." He leans down and kisses me briefly before heading into the kitchen. "Thank you for brewing the coffee!"

"He's still talking but walking away from his phone, so I'm gonna put

the volume up," I call to my ex-step-
uncle.

"All right," he calls back, and I hear the fridge open and close. He's making breakfast. I haven't even thought about eating yet. "If he starts being noisy maybe it'll wake those two up finally."

"He plays music sometimes," I reply. I glance back and he's moved his phone, and now is standing in front of some kind of workout equipment. I get back to my paperwork, this one a little bit more advanced than the others, so I need to pay extra attention, unfortunately not paying attention to the livestream.

Until the noises start.

"What the *fuck* are you watching, little girl?" Daddy asks, stumbling down the stairs. "We can hear it up in the bedroom."

I glance at my phone, and it no longer sounds like a musician on livestream but rather live porn as he moans, groans, grunts, and gasps.

"Sounds like she's getting a good show," Uncle Tony calls from the kitchen. "They let that stuff get streamed like that now?"

My face heats up and I lower the volume as the man gasps and kneels before the screen.

"*I'm not done,*" he declares, voice ragged, and at that moment Nonno also makes his appearance.

"Il piccolo, even you have to think it's too early to be watching stuff like that," he scolds amusedly. As if I'm the only sex addict in the house.

"He's working out! Alone!" I say hastily. But my face and now my ears are still heated up. I guess it doesn't matter how old I am, or how many times I let the three men use me any way they wish: being raised by them makes me a little shy when my clothes are on.

"Baby, if people sound like that while working out, I'm surprised every public gym hasn't turned into an orgy," Daddy comments, sitting on the couch behind me and pulling me to him, back to front.

I close my eyes and lean into his strong embrace, smelling the coffee he holds in his free hand.

"We could build a gym in-house and find out?" I suggest, looking back and giving him my best innocent puppy eyes.

He arches an eyebrow. "We've had sex in every room of this house. You want to add another?"

I shrug. "I like a challenge."

Uncle Tony laughs as he enters the living room again. "Tesoro, shut down the man auditioning for the next Passionflix movie and come eat breakfast."

I mute my phone but don't leave the live — I'd never do that — and join my men at the kitchen table. We have a gorgeous dining room we often use at dinner, but breakfast and lunch are always in the kitchen when we're home for both meals. We're usually too busy and exhausted to clean up a full dining setup all the time, even on weekends.

Uncle Tony is the best cook out of all of us, though we're all pretty good. But when we can, we leave it to him.

Today he made caprese omelets with flash fried potato wedges and strawberries dusted with sugar.

"You spoil us," I tell him, kissing him softly.

"You all deserve it," he replies.

I help Uncle Tony plate the food and bring it to the table, getting a third cup of coffee along the way.

"You need all that caffeine?" Daddy comments.

"I have three boyfriends, I need the stamina," I reply cutely.

"fiancés," Uncle Tony corrects. "Even if you can only marry one of us on paper."

I smile thinking about it. Not that we're in a hurry down the aisle. My men proposed to me six months ago at Nam San Tower, by the Love Locks, in Seoul. It was decided I'd marry Uncle Tony, since he is the only one out of the three who hasn't yet been married.

And marrying my mom's ex-husband or his dad would send some strange signals to many people. Not that marrying his fraternal twin brother won't.

Another reason we are in no rush. The *drama*...

Maybe we brought this on ourselves, but shit happens. Especially years after a divorce and nearly two years of not seeing them at all. Then of course getting closer due to stalkers and a little murder.

Just an average romance, right?

Uncle Tony and Daddy leave after breakfast to meet with clients, even though we're not supposed to do meetings on weekends. Some clients get particular treatment.

It's mid-afternoon by the time the mail comes, and by then I am desperately bored and, let's be honest, still a little turned on by that workout this morning.

I sort through the letters — seriously, we're supposed to be paperless by now — and then check the few packages. Some photocards, a lamp, a new figurine I ordered, and ... something from a sex shop?

And it's in my name. I did not order anything, but my name isn't common, so it can't exactly be a mistake. Slicing the tape open, I pull out a box with a vibrator that is apparently app-controlled.

Just as I go to call out, soft footsteps come behind me.

"Anything good, il piccolina?" Nonno asks, leaning against the foyer threshold. His eyebrow arches and his smirk goes higher on the right, a sure sign he's amused.

"You tell me," I reply. His silver hair is damp from his shower, tendrils clinging to the sides of his face and sharp jaw, bangs slicked back. His red shorts and white Calvin Klein tee still smell like white tea and lily fabric softener, which mixes well with his clean soap scent.

"It came," is all he says.

"Yes, it did," I reply. "The question is, why did you order it? I haven't exactly needed to use any toys since you three are always ready and willing to break me off anytime I ask … and sometimes even when I don't."

He has the nerve to look sheepish for a second, but I don't buy the coy charm. Hell, I haven't bought into that for a long time. Especially not when his eyes sparkle with mischief.

"Well, yeah," he replies, taking the box from my hands and extracting the cone-shaped toy. I'm almost ashamed to admit I haven't seen one that looks like this. He must notice the confusion on my face and he grins. "What?"

"That doesn't look ... right," I comment.

He takes his phone and types as he replies, "Oh, bambino, that's probably because it doesn't go where you think it does."

I'm sorry? I open my mouth to say something and, for once, I am rendered speechless.

"Little one..." He moves closer, toy dangling between two fingers and his phone in his palm as the other hand reaches out to brush my long, dark hair from my face. Just that soft touch has me nearly melting into him. "Do you trust me?"

I nod. "Of course."

"Let me make you scream then." His lips ghost across mine and he cocks his head. "Bed. Naked. Now." He smacks my ass as I walk past him, strong palm easily making the skin sting even through my clothes.

I put my clothes in the hamper because I know I'll need another shower after he's done with me. He didn't say how he wants me on the bed, so I perch on the edge as he comes in, the toy freshly cleaned and suddenly without a shirt or shorts, just in his dark gray Calvins. He's so hard, he's straining the fabric and I crave to taste him. But that's not on his mind this time.

"Lay down for me," he says. "Spread your legs. Let me taste what's mine first."

I shiver at his words, reminding me that I do belong to him, completely, and do as he asks.

He leans over me, his lips ghosting down my neck, my chest, sucking first one nipple and then the other. With these light, erotic touches, he turns me into an absolute mess. And he's not even trying.

He kisses down my stomach, teeth nipping at my navel, before he kneels down before the bed and spreads my legs open farther, strong hands ensuring I can't move. Not that I want to, but there's something sexy about being restrained this way, held in his grasp.

His lips kiss my already sensitive clit, then his tongue dips inside, finding me already wet. It's not even an exaggeration, sometimes just a look from any of my men will have me needing to change my panties after a few minutes.

His tongue teases with a few soft licks at first, and as always my body gets falsely complacent before he flicks my clit and dives deeper inside, tasting me as if I'm his favorite treat. In this position, his nose brushes my clit, not enough pressure to get me off but enough to drive me insane.

"Ah, Nonno," I gasp out, my arm thrown over my face.

He moves back enough to say, "Eyes on me. You know this by now." His deep voice vibrates against me and I whimper but do as he says, propping myself on my elbows as I watch his talented tongue get back to work. He can argue in court and win the most impossible cases, but only I get to know what else his mouth is good for, and a surge of smug pride rushes through me.

His eyes meet mine and he must see the expression on my face change because he moves, his tongue now working my clit and he easily slides two strong fingers inside me, curling and moving them just right.

I come without warning, crying out his name as he works me through it, using just his fingers this time. Wetness soaks my thighs and his hand, and he wipes his face with the back of his free hand, watching me.

Eventually, when I feel boneless and soaked, he removes his fingers, sucking on them as I watch. As if I didn't just climax, my pussy clenches again at the sight.

He gently moves my legs so I'm laying on the bed proper and, gentler than last time, taps my ass. "Turn over, present for me, il piccolina. We're not done."

I do as he asks, knowing from his words and the fact he has that toy with him, I'm in for a long afternoon.

When the others get back, they're going to be so jealous.

He runs his fingers through my wetness, coating them, before I feel his fingers at my rear hole.

He stretches me, using my own wetness as lube, and I wriggle back against him, earning me another smack on my ass. "Wanton little thing," he comments.

I feel the cold silicone of the plug run against my folds now; he's coating it in my juices, taking his time, teasing me back to being absolutely ready for him again.

He removes the toy and I feel the tip against my ass. "Hold still," he croons, his other hand on the small of my back, both keeping me from moving and giving me comfort. "It'll hurt at first, baby. But I know you like the pain."

He eases it in, getting to the widest part of the base. I'm absolutely dripping between my legs, desperate for him to fill me up, when there's a burst of pain as the toy slides fully in me, filling me perfectly if a bit too much since I'm not used to it.

Then it begins to vibrate, and I nearly lose my position on my knees and yelp.

He laughs as I try to get acclimated to the new sensation, enjoying the arousal and discomfort.

"Good girl," he says, and he moves a little, before I feel the blunt tip of his cock at my entrance. "*My* good girl."

He slides deep inside with no resistance, filling me completely, perfectly. We fall into a familiar rhythm, one that never ever gets old, as his hands roughly grip my hips, fingers leaving bruises that never fully heal. Not that I want them to.

He fucks me hard and slow, giving and getting pleasure, driving me to the brink and back. His breathing is rough, loud in my ears, louder than even my whimpers and little cries every time he hits that spot that makes me see stars.

This is why I haven't needed any toys. Who would want one when these three men I have can take me to heights of pleasure I never imagined were real?

He grinds into me, hips rough and pressing his hard cock deeper than the ocean. It's close to painful but it's a delicious pain that nearly sends me over the edge again, but just as I'm about to crest, he pulls out of me.

I can't help it, I whine.

"Oh, cute," he coos, almost mockingly. "But I'm still not done. Understand?"

I nod. "Yes, sir."

The toy turns off, and I feel my body relax a little.

Mistake.

He pulls it out in one tug, leaving me suddenly empty and my body adjusting to the sting of pain that vanishes as fast as it comes. His cock, now just as covered in my wetness as the plug had been, presses against the slightly gaping hole, but it's still not big enough, exactly, as he pushes into me slowly.

The ragged sounds of his breath let me know how much he's loving this, and that even *his* stamina is being threatened.

"Fuck, Nonno," I gasp.

"You like how that feels?" he asks. "You like being my little toy for the day?"

"Mm, yes, I do," I say, but it's more of a whine. I need to come. I need him all the way inside me. I need him to finish ruining me. "Please..."

"Fuck me I love how you beg, princess," he says, moving more deliberately, and then he's completely inside me, filling me.

Then he starts to move.

"So tight, you were made for me," he says, thrusting hard enough the bed begins to shake, headboard hitting the wall with every thrust and primal grunt that follows.

I cry out, a high sound I don't think I've ever made before as he fucks my ass harder and faster than he was just now in my pussy. He's relentless, rhythmic, perfect, taking me closer and closer to the edge.

"Nonno, please," I beg. I need just a little more. A little more from him. I need him to take me higher.

He doesn't seem to listen to me, and the longer he goes, the more intense everything feels. I can feel every ridge of his cock against my sensitive and (slightly) lesser used walls, the sweat that drips from him onto me.

Before I can beg again, one hand lets my hips go and he rubs my clit hard, rolling it between his fingers, and I lose every ounce of control I possess and come hard, squirting on his hand.

His breaths get more ragged and he gasps my name as I feel him fill me with his hot cum.

We stay like that for a moment, coming down from our dual highs, before he gently pulls out of my painful and used hole.

I said I wanted to be ruined.

He did not disappoint.

I slip bonelessly from his grasp and he comes to lay next to me, breathing so hard his chest rises and falls like he just performed a concert or something.

He gathers me to him, his sweat-slicked skin warm against mine, and kisses me hard.

"Like it?" he murmurs.

"Mmhm," I mumble, too tired to speak.

"Good. You'll be ready for round two soon when my boys get home."

Chapter Two

Sasha

 DID A round two. And then a round three before bed, where I nearly collapsed from exhaustion. A perfect Saturday, if you ask me.

The last thing anyone wants is their phone ringing at ass o'clock in the morning. Especially when they're exhausted from a night of sex. I don't even check who it is, just see that it's half past seven and fling my phone somewhere on the mattress and hope nobody crushes it.

Then Daddy's phone begins to ring.

"Fuck, that better not be a client," Uncle Tony comments, scrubbing his hand along his dark blond goatee.

"Gina," Daddy says.

My mother.

His ex-wife.

She'd never call this early on a Sunday. Hell, she'd never be awake. I nearly leap in bed, my heart in my throat. Did something happen to one of my younger half-siblings?

"Answer it, stunad," Nonno mutters.

"Gina? Everything okay?" Daddy asks when he answers. There's silence. "So you and the kids are okay?" He lets out a sigh and his rigid body goes lax. "Did you just call Sasha? I thought I heard her phone ring down the hall." He winks at me. "Give me a minute and let me get her." He makes a noisy show of pretending to get out of bed and walk to "my" bedroom. He knocks on the headboard as if it's a door. "Sasha, get up. Your mother is on the phone."

I bite my lip so laughter doesn't escape and whack Uncle Tony, who begins to giggle as well. He buries his face into a pillow.

"Mom?" I don't have to fake the sleepiness in my voice. "Are you okay? What about Caleb and Maggie?"

"They're fine. I'm fine." Mom often sounds stiff. This is stiffer than usual.

What the Hell happened?

"Then what made you call me at practically dawn? You're never up this early," I tell her.

"It's your grandmother."

Nonna, Nonno's wife, died before I was born, when Daddy and Uncle Tony were teenagers. And I never knew my mom's mom at all.

"Your mother?" I ask, to be sure.

"She died."

* * *

And that's how Daddy and I wound up at Mom's house, where I grew up, where she and Daddy spent their married years, and where my siblings still live.

I'm not sure how to treat Mom. Is she sad? She doesn't look sad. She looks shocked and, honestly, a little pissed off. But then, she often looks pissed off.

Mom hasn't seen her mother since she was eighteen. When Mom got pregnant out of wedlock, her devoutly religious mom kicked her out, not believing that Mom had been raped.

"And even if she had," Mom once said, "she still would've kicked me out."

I've seen pictures of her when Mom was a kid, a pretty, petite woman with a severe bun (sort of like what Mom wears now) and a really ugly muumuu all the time. But I never personally heard from her. I was most likely considered a mistake, an abomination.

Mom stares at the TV, which is playing a variety show I introduced my sister to, the happy, laughing people at odds with our current situation. I really should turn it off, but I don't want to move.

Tension cuts through the air, and I touch my chest, where my engagement ring rests on a chain around my neck. No one knows I'm engaged yet, and I prefer it that way for now. But I like to keep it here, the slight weight a reminder of how loved I truly am.

"What can we do for you, Gina?" Daddy asks her, caring even though their relationship has been anything but good since a couple years before they divorced.

"It's not me who needs anything done," she replies, and I furrow my eyebrows. She glances at me. "It's you."

"Come again?"

Mom moves a manila envelope towards me. "As the closest living relative, I am the unfortunate executor of my mother's will. She never appointed anyone. And her lawyer came and delivered it, along with the news, this morning."

I take the envelope, almost afraid to open it.

"You can read it," Mom tells me.

I do, noticing very few people are listed. Apparently my grandmother didn't like anybody.

"To my estranged daughter Gina, I leave the house she grew up in. In all likelihood, she needs it."

Oh, that was rude. Like she thought Mom would be some kind of vagabond or something. Mom is the VP at a huge cosmetics company; she didn't even need Daddy's money when they first met. She had already been doing well for herself.

"I hope you either burn it or sell it," I tell Mom.

Mom nods tersely. "Burning it would be too much trouble. I already called the realtor Tony uses." She makes an impatient gesture with her hands. "Go on."

I read down, reading family member names I didn't even know existed until now. Some got money, some got stocks, some got jewelry.

Then, there at the bottom:

"To my only, ill-gotten grandchild, Sasha, I leave five million dollars to ensure she has a good future. However, this inheritance comes with stipulations:

"She will have an education by now or enroll in university. She will also be married or engaged to be married before the inheritance will be released to her. Should she falsify an engagement, the inheritance will be revoked. The inheritance will be held in trust until such time as expectations are met."

What. The. Fuck?

I don't realize I say it out loud until Mom replies, "That sums it up pretty well."

"Can I read it?" Daddy asks, looking between Mom and me, and we both nod. He takes it and I can see an odd mixture of disgust and amusement in his eyes before he shakes his head and places the will on the coffee table. "She wanted to ensure Sasha…"

Mom scoffs. "Didn't end up a pregnant bum like her mother. You can say it."

"Mom, no. What my grandmother thought couldn't be further from the truth," I say. "Yeah, so apparently I need to be a 'respectable woman' in her eyes before I can get the money. What she doesn't understand is you were never the person she made you out to be, and that's on her."

I look back down at the will and say, "Maggie and Caleb didn't get anything?"

Daddy cuts in, "Chances are, she didn't know they exist."

"I'll give them mine. I don't want it." Nor do I need it. I have a fantastic job as a recent law school graduate and am with three extremely wealthy men.

Mom smiles a little. "You have to get married first. The way you work ... it's unlikely you'll find anyone. Especially if you don't move out on your own soon."

I steadfastly don't meet Daddy's eyes. "My career is important. More than dating."

Mom smiles at that. "If I instilled anything good in you, it's that. Though when you do get married, I'll be a blubbering mess."

"Who's getting married? Dad!"

My younger half-sister Maggie is still half asleep, but she shakes off the tiredness to run and hug her dad — her biological dad. He hugs her back and Mom rolls her eyes at the "dramatics" as she always calls it whenever Maggie or I get excited about things. Granted, Maggie probably doesn't see Daddy enough between work, our relationship, and her AP classes. At eighteen, she's already got acceptances into the best universities for when summer hits.

"Daddy, are you getting married?" she asks, standing up.

Once more, I don't meet his eyes. Technically I'm not legally marrying him, so it's not a lie when he says, "No, sweetie, we were talking about your sister, hypothetically."

"He's suddenly too busy to date," Mom pipes up. "Your brother too, for that matter. He used to come into the sales floor and chat up all the young girls. He hasn't been in for ages. Did it finally stop working?"

"Mom!" Maggie and I cry at once. Maggie giggles, while my face turns crimson. That's my fiancé she's talking about! And I can assure everyone, *it* definitely still works.

Daddy nearly chokes on spit and says, "Really, Gina, come on. He's grown up ... finally. That's all."

Mom chuckles. "Never thought I'd see the day." She glances at me and adds, "Just do me a favor, honey, and don't go trying to date any of your stepfamily's friends. They're all as bad as your Uncle Tony."

I grin. "I wouldn't dream of it."

"Oh, there's one more thing…" Mom trails off and points to the very bottom line of the will, right above my grandmother's signature.

"All heirs are required to attend my funeral proceedings. My daughter, being executor, does not need to. My lawyer, however, will ensure everyone else attends, or they forfeit their inheritance."

Shit. Guess I've got a funeral to go to.

Chapter Three

Tony

I CAN'T REMEMBER the last time I laughed so hard.

"Wait. Wait. You get five million bucks, but you gotta be married or ready to be married. And you can't tell anyone you're engaged yet because it's to your ex-step-uncle. AKA me." I burst into another peal of laughter. "That's fucking nuts."

Sasha gives me a small smile, looking amused at my amusement. "And we have to attend the funeral."

"We?" Gene says, looking at her.

"I'm not going alone," she replies. "I need my men with me."

"I hate funerals," I comment. "There's always drama."

"I'm just gonna show my face, make sure the lawyer sees me, spit on her corpse, and leave."

That's my girl. Same girl who wanted us to fuck on her abusive ex's grave. She hasn't changed, despite growing up, graduating law school, and generally being the sexiest motherfucker I have ever known.

To say I am proud to call myself hers is an understatement.

Gene sighs and stands. "I have to go meet with the PR team of the guy who crashed his electric scooter into the cop car. See you guys at dinner."

Dad is already in his meetings. He takes the more elite business clients; Gene does entertainment predominantly; I do sports. And we all

take criminal cases as well. Though once
Sasha makes partner, she will head that
department.

Did I mention she's smart as Hell
and I love it? Today, she's helping me on
my cases, handling filing and reports
while I handle Zoom meetings and write
up the aforementioned reports.

She takes cases, but she's still a
junior here, and every time one of us
gets a case that has things that are new
to her, we keep her at our respective
sides.

Not that any of us mind.

The case I'm working on is in
defense of a local basketball player who
cheated on his wife, who now wants half
his salary from the NBA. And the NBA
has no rules in place to stop that from
happening.

Personally? I hate cheaters and think he shouldn't win the case. But I still have a job to do. I'm typing up my final closing arguments to present to the judge when I begin to let my mind wander.

Sasha says she doesn't want the inheritance for herself; she'll split it between her two younger half-siblings, my blood-related niece and nephew. She still needs to be married to claim it, though. And despite what I say, despite what she, Gene, and Dad believe, the fact that her mother would lose her shit over our marriage and the fact we are all in a relationship with each other is not why I keep delaying making plans.

I'm so lost in my reverie I don't notice Sasha has moved until she's behind me, her hands on my shoulders.

Her palms are warm even under my vest and shirt.

"Uncle Tony, what's wrong?" Her voice is soft, breath warm against my ear.

"It's nothing, tesoro," I say.

"You're an awful liar." Her hands squeeze my shoulders. "You're not this tense because of the sleazy basketball player."

The little massage feels incredible and I close my eyes to savor it, letting out a little groan as her talented hands work away the knots I just made pop up.

"I love that sound," she says, then her hands move up my neck, and to my ponytail. She takes my hair down and her nails rake over my scalp, both relaxing and exciting me at the same time.

"Tesoro..." I warn.

"I'm not doing anything!" she protests, her voice an octave higher.

"You lost the right to act like you're innocent the moment you flashed that sweet cunt at me on the sidewalk after you let your ex steal your panties."

"Pretend I am." Her whisper is near my ear, and I want nothing more than to bury myself in her warm mouth and teach her what happens when you tease me.

Before I can, though, her arms wind around me, her hands clasped over my heart. Her chin is tucked into my shoulder, where it meets my neck, and she gives a little sigh.

"Please talk to me. Maybe I can't help, but you don't have to deal with whatever it is all alone."

Fuck. I love her too much sometimes. I don't deserve her. And that's the problem.

"Tesoro ... if you want the truth, I feel inadequate."

"What? Why?"

I place one of my hands over both of hers on my chest before I speak further. "I was never a good man. You know that firsthand. I changed because I fell in love with you deeper than I imagined possible. But that doesn't change my past, the person I am somewhere deep down.

"You deserve better than me as your husband."

She's silent for a moment before her voice, barely audible, asks, "Why would you say that about yourself?" She hugs me tighter, burying her face in my hair.

"There's something I never told you. Something I hate myself for. And I'm afraid you'll hate me too once I tell you."

It's not just her who doesn't know. No one does. I'm sure Gene guessed, but that's not the same as knowing.

"Did you cheat on me? On us?" Her voice is so small.

"Never," I vow.

"Then tell me."

I take a breath and begin to speak.

"Do you remember the time you brought your friend to one of my summer parties, the last one you came to before your mother divorced Gene?"

I feel her nod against my neck. "She called you a DILF. I got mad at her."

"Why?"

She's quiet before saying, "Because you were mine. Even if I didn't know it yet. You and Daddy and Nonno. You all belonged to me."

Maybe this won't be so hard.

"That day ... I don't know what was different. Something changed. In you, in me, in the stars. I don't know. But I saw you, really *saw* you, for the first time. I couldn't take my eyes off you. Or my thoughts. I was hard as a rock, and none of the women I'd invited held my interest. All I wanted was you.

"I needed relief, and here is where I should lie and say I was on autopilot or something, but I love you too much to lie to you. I was very aware of what I was doing as I went into my house and the guest room you used to change your clothes into your swimsuit.

"You left everything folded neatly, I remember that. Your panties were on top, and I picked them up; they were as soft as I imagined your skin would be. It didn't take three minutes before I covered them in my cum, wishing it was you. I left them on top, just as you had them, knowing they'd be dry by the time you put them back on to leave."

There. That's it. My most shameful secret, out in the open. My greatest sin; the main reason I will surely burn in Hell and deserve it. Compounded by the fact that recounting the day has made me just as hard.

Sasha is silent, then her hands move off of me, slipping from my grip. My stomach sinks somewhere down where my knees should be, and there's a knot in my chest.

Did I lose her?

Her heels click on the floor as she steps around to stand before me, looking down at me. Her eyes are hooded, and her cheeks are pink.

"Tesoro..."

"Shh." Her response is sharp and I don't know what to make of it.

Before I can ponder her intentions, she sinks before me, her pretty face level with the cock straining in my pants. When she looks up at me, her amber brown eyes are filled with fire.

I'm afraid to speak.

Her manicured hands reach for my belt, and I let her, still a little confused. A part of me wonders if she's going to get my letter opener and stab me there. She would if she wanted to, I know that. That thought, though, doesn't keep my cock from bouncing free as soon as it has room. I'm so horny, a little stabbing might even get me off.

Finally, she speaks.

"I was *sixteen*."

"I know." My voice is rough, and I don't know what she might do next. Maybe it should be obvious, but it shocks the shit out of me when she wraps her pretty pink lips around the head of my cock and sucks. My upper head falls back onto the chair and I grip the arms tightly. Normally I'd be holding her hair, but this time I'm content to let her do her thing.

Just like that day ten years ago, I don't last long, coming hard in her mouth while I moan her name.

Her lips leave me, and then her hand is in my hair, pulling my head up. She leans over me, and kisses me, her tongue probing my lips open.

My seed slips from her mouth to mine, and while we've done this with my father and brother's, she's never done it with mine. Not to me, anyway.

I swallow, the perverseness of this whole afternoon sinking into my soul, damning me further.

But if my Sasha will smirk at me with this fire in her eyes always, I will happily go to Hell over and over again.

"It's only fair, Uncle," she quips. "I wasn't expecting your cum then, and you weren't expecting it now."

I pull her to my lap, careful of my cock, and kiss her once more. "You're as twisted as I am, aren't you?"

She arches an eyebrow. "It took you this long to figure that out?" She tucks herself into my chest, my chin resting on her head. "Now, I never ever want to hear you say you won't be a good husband, or whatever bullshit you just spewed. I love you, and nothing, not even your perverted mind, will change that. You're mine."

I kiss the top of her head, smelling her perfume and floral shampoo.

"I'm yours."

Chapter Four

Sasha

A S I ZIP up the back of my black lace dress, I smile at myself in the mirror. The front plunges down, and the fabric covering my breasts is reinforced to keep them upright. The lacy hem reaches mid-thigh, and I wear strappy black stiletto sandals and an old fashioned black hat with netting, which is pinned to my hair.

I look hot.

Much too hot for a funeral, and I hope my late grandmother is already spinning in her casket at how I'm dressed to go to her final farewell.

My men are all in expensive, custom suits, and Uncle Tony, as usual, has eschewed a tie, his wild curls wrestled into a ponytail. Daddy's tie is bright red and I want to laugh. People are definitely not going to be happy with my little crew.

The funeral home is in the suburbs right outside Chicago, and I haven't been here in about twenty years, since I was a small child. It smells like perfume and too many decaying flowers, and the hum of hushed voices grates on my ears.

Daddy checks the notice board and points us in the direction of the proper chapel and I walk with my head held high. Despite our differences, I am my mother's daughter, and I need to represent her as well as myself.

The chapel is full; most people are Daddy's age and older, which makes me stand out.

As well as four others not much older than me, whom I recognize.

"Did ... we ask the Kangs to be here?" Nonno asks his sons.

Daddy and Uncle Tony shake their heads.

I approach Julie Kang, the wife of the three Kang brothers, who run the Chicago chapter of the kkangpae.

"Sasha Santini," she says when she spots me. At 5'8" she towers over me, even in my heels, and is just as intimidating as her husbands are. "How did you know my cunt of a great aunt?"

I pause, mouth open, unable to speak. "What?"

"I'm not here because funerals are fun," she comments.

"That's my grandmother," I blurt out. "I never met her but ..."

"You were in the will." Julie gives a wan smile. "I hadn't seen her since I was twelve; the Marconi side of the family disowned hers. So you're my cousin's kid then? Gina?"

I nod and Julie shakes her head.

"Small fucking world," one of her husbands says. The one with the tattoos. "We had to prove our marriage was legal before Julie could collect."

"They let you have it even with three husbands?" I ask.

She nods. "It says I have to be married and educated. It never said I had to be monogamous."

The tall one with the dyed blond hair shrugs. "She's only legally married to Han-ji anyway."

Ah, that is the tattooed guy's name. I'm not around them enough to remember the three men by name, and barely by sight, but Julie saved my life when my biological psycho-rapist-murderer father blackmailed me into meeting him and tried to kidnap me.

Wow, my family is really not normal, are we?

"I suppose you should pay your respects, piccolina," Nonno says, gesturing to the open casket at the head of the room, suspended on a dias and surrounded by flowers.

I grimace, but that is why I am here. I need to be seen at the funeral, sign the registry, and ensure I can at least have the inheritance on hold for me.

Until I get married. Which may cause more issues than anything else.

My men stay behind me as I walk to the casket and see my maternal grandmother for the very first time in my life.

First real life look at her, and she's a corpse. Not many people can say that.

She looks like the one photograph Mom had but shriveled. Her jowls sag, her neck sags, her arms in the black dress she's wearing are sagging. Her face is set in a scowl; usually undertakers make the corpse look peaceful. I don't think this lady could look anything but pissed off. They tried to fix that with makeup, but she looks like a painted clown from Hell.

"Goodbye, you old hag," I comment, glaring. I make the Sign of the Cross over her like a good Catholic. "Hope Hell is hot enough for you."

Uncle Tony chokes back a laugh, and Daddy nudges him, just within my line of sight.

I turn on my heel and sign the registry before exiting the visiting hall, my dutiful, wonderful men in tow. The man who runs the funeral home nods to me, and I politely nod back, but barely pay attention to him.

Maybe it is all the emotion, but I feel … crazy. A good kinda crazy. Julie already got her inheritance despite it being noted she's technically married to three men as well, and my first look at my grandmother was her overly made up, saggy, pale corpse.

I need my emotions centered, and for me, there is only one way to do that.

"Where are you leading us, tesoro?" Uncle Tony asks.

I'm not sure. I'll know it when I see it.

And then I do see it. A chapel open as a display, for mourners to visit and see what a basic funeral/wake setup looks like. No one is in here, as it's Sunday, and they don't do bookings on Sundays on account of needing staff to be available for the funerals and the families.

I grab Daddy, who is closest to me, and drag him into the room, and the other two men, of course, follow.

"Shut the door, please," I tell Nonno, who is in the rear.

"Tesoro..." Uncle Tony's voice has a hint of warning in it but also amusement.

"Oh, tell me you're not thinking..." Daddy trails off as he

watches me hop onto the top of the closed gray casket in the display room.

I eye each of my men and say, "I don't care which of you, or if all of you do it, someone is getting me off right here, right now."

"Bossy all of a sudden, isn't she?" Uncle Tony comments.

"Maybe we should show her what ordering us around does," Daddy muses.

A flush of heat suffuses me at the way they look at me.

"I'll go first," Uncle Tony offers, walking towards me, not taking his eyes from mine. He hikes my dress up, seeing I'm not wearing panties. "Oh, you had this planned, didn't you?"

I shake my head. "Not exactly, just being hopeful." Before I can finish the last syllable, he slaps my bare and already dripping pussy, and I yelp.

"Stai zitto!" Nonno scolds, effectively shutting me up, even as Uncle Tony bends down and licks a stripe from hole to clit.

"You always taste so good, the embodiment of sin," Tony says with a rasp before going back to feasting on me.

I toss my head back and try to control my breathing so I don't yell out as he fucks me with his tongue, tasting me like he hasn't eaten in years. Gripping his hair with one hand, the other braces me on the casket so I don't lose my balance.

An orgasm is ripped out of me before I can even blink, and he keeps eating me out, giving me another as I'm still coming down from the first one.

I can't control the sounds I make; I can't even try.

Uncle Tony stands up, wiping my wetness off his lips and chin and if I could come again so quickly, that would do it. As would the sight of the obvious tents in his, Daddy's, and Nonno's pants.

"Set her down. Looks like we need to show her how to keep her mouth shut," Daddy comments, and Uncle Tony does as he says, setting me onto my knees on the threadbare, poorly patterned carpet.

Daddy and Nonno free their cocks, and Nonno grabs me by the hair, directing me first to his, then Daddy's cock. I do my best to suck and lick, but they're not interested in anything but using my mouth as a masturbation tool. The thought makes me clit throb as more wetness slicks my thighs.

Daddy comes first, and I choke as I swallow it all down, making little noises in my throat as tears prick my eyes.

That spurs Nonno on, and he follows suit down my throat, and I relish the sweet and salty taste of them both on my tongue.

"Hold her still," Uncle Tony says, and I see his hard cock being stroked in a veiny hand. Not his. It's Nonno's hand jerking him off over me.

Daddy holds me and Uncle Tony comes with a rasp, covering my chest.

"Good girl," Nonno praises.

I want to come again but even my reckless ass knows we should get out of here before that happens. I stand on shaky legs and reach for my clutch to get a tissue.

"No," Uncle Tony commands.

"You're going to walk out of here wearing his cum on your pretty tits," Daddy adds.

"Show everyone you're an owned little slut," Nonno finishes.

Fuck, I really love them.

Chapter Five

Nonno

DESPITE COMING FROM a superstitious country, I am not generally a superstitious man. I don't believe in signs and omens; I don't worry if a black cat crosses my path. However, I also believe in trusting your gut, as Americans like to say.

And today, the morning after the funeral, I feel like my gut has been put in the washing machine.

It's at breakfast Sasha makes an announcement.

"I want to do something," she says. "But I need all three of you to promise me you won't deviate from what I say."

Gene scoffs. "And what makes you think you can give us orders, hmm?"

She grins. "Listen to what I want first, and I won't have to order you to do anything."

"You seem awfully confident of that, tesoro," Tony says, leaning back in his recliner. "But you've piqued my interest."

"Mine too," I reply. "Though ever since you had us fuck you on your ex's grave, I've been a little apprehensive any time you suggest something new."

Our sweet girl bursts into laughter. "It's nothing as morbid as that."

Gene leans in and whispers to his twin, "Why don't I believe her?"

"So, I won't put it cutely or whatever, I'd rather just say what I want. I want you guys to roofie me and film yourselves fucking me."

My fairly unflappable Anthony Jr. nearly chokes on his coffee.

"Piccolina, do you have any idea how illegal that is?" I ask.

"I'm not a random girl in a bar, Nonno. I'm quite literally asking for it," she points out.

Gene rubs his forehead and I wonder how much trouble this girl and her overly logical, yet diabolical, mind gave him when he was raising her. "Can we table this discussion for when we don't have to rush off to work? There's a lot that needs to go into this. Dosage, what we'll use, when, where, your signing a consent form as a formality..." He trails off.

Sasha, clearly seeing she's won, smiles. "Sure, Daddy. We can talk over dinner tonight instead."

I chuckle. "Madone. You don't give up, huh?"

"I may not be blood, but I am your granddaughter."

Well ... what the Hell do I say to that? She's right.

We get ready to head into work, all taking one car this time since none of us have off-site meetings. Environmentally friendly, as Sasha likes to say. She also likes to say that when she makes one or more of us shower with her.

As soon as we get to our offices, which make up the top floors of the building we own, I know something isn't right. It's too quiet. While we aren't a loud workplace, there are always phones ringing, copiers going off, and people talking.

It's silent as a grave.

"Is it weird or is it just me?" Sasha asks, and I feel her gripping my suit jacket from behind, like she used to do when she was a child.

"Very fucking weird," Anthony Jr says.

"I have the creeps," Eugene admits.

"Come with me to my office," I command, and all three listen to me and follow me to the end of the hall on the top floor.

My secretary looks like she's seen a ghost, sitting behind her desk with her face ashen and eyes wide.

"Paola," I greet. "Has something happened?"

She stands, not wanting me to come near her. "Mr. Santini, sir, with all due respect, I quit. But I figured I should stay here until you arrived to tell you why, and why many clients have called in and canceled all representation from this firm."

"Che cazzo?" I blurt out, not usually one to curse at work. At least, not where anyone can hear me.

She turns her computer monitor to face me, and I feel lightheaded.

The pictures displayed there, sent in what looks like a mass email to our staff and clientele, show Sasha, Eugene, Anthony Jr, and myself.

Yesterday.

In the funeral home.

Our cocks out and covering Sasha in cum.

How could this happen?

"Paola, please don't—"

She holds a hand up. "I don't want to hear what you have to say. I'm leaving!" Getting out from behind the desk, she stalks past us, and none of us even glance back at her. Our eyes are fixed on the screen.

Faster than I thought I could still move, I enter my office proper and turn on the computer. Buried under cancelation emails from clients is the offending email, with the subject line, "THIS IS JUST THE BEGINNING".

The pictures attached show Anthony Jr licking Sasha on top of the coffin, and each one of us surrounding her as she lay on the floor, breasts bare, covering her in our cum. One shot clearly shows my hand wrapped around my son's cock as I bring him to completion.

"Nonno, tell me I'm dreaming."
Sasha looks pale, and she plops down in
one of my guest chairs as if her legs can't
hold her anymore.

I read the email aloud.

"If we do not receive the five
million dollars Sasha Santini inherited
from her late grandmother within
twenty-four hours, these pictures will go
out to the press and other media, not
just to your clients and family."

"Family?" Now it is Eugene's turn
to look terrified, even as he gently rubs
Sasha's back, trying to calm her down.

Anthony Jr comes behind me and
looks over my shoulder. "Shit shit shit.
Gene ... Gina's email is on this list. No
one was BCC'd."

"No..." Sasha covers her face with
her hands.

This was what we desperately tried to hide for all these years since Sasha was eighteen: our relationship. This was why she delayed marrying any of us for so long. Because we needed to be sure it was spun properly to the press and keep the fact that my sons and I are also in a relationship together a secret.

"What do we do?" Sasha gasps, trembling. She's ready to cry.

I glare at my computer, as if I could curse the people who did this with my eyes alone.

"We do what we always have done, piccolina. We fight. And we survive."

Chapter Six

Gene

I HAVE TO be insane.

At least, that's what I tell myself as I stand outside the front door where I used to live, where my ex wife and our two children remain. I have to confront Gina about the pictures before she comes to me, or before she does something rash. Were she to go to court and try and get Caleb to no longer have visitation rights with me, I'd be devastated. Maggie is eighteen, but Gina could still sway her to have an unfortunate opinion of me.

Tony told me I was nuts, too, for going. He bet me a month's worth of blow jobs she'll completely lose her shit on me.

My brother is probably going to win that bet, but no skin off my nose. Not like it would be the first time or the last I sucked his cock and enjoyed it.

Hence why we are in this mess.

Sasha was distraught all day, but helped us contact and placate clients and employees alike. She was a saint, and she saved us from going insane. Well, she saved me, anyway.

Especially since now I have to face my ex-wife. Her mother.

I still have a key. In case of emergencies. This time, though, I ring the doorbell. It's evening, and I know Gina is home from work. Caleb isn't here; he's on a trip for the week with his school. Maggie's room looks dark. Hopefully she's not home either.

The door opens to reveal my furious ex-wife. Her eyes are practically glowing with rage. So they did send her the videos and photos. Meaning they probably sent them to others we know as well as the clients who terminated contracts with us today. Quietly ruining us before someone goes to the press.

Fan-fucking-tastic.

"Gina—"

I don't even see the slap coming. One second I'm speaking, the next the left side of my face is on fire. Even the sound seems to hit afterwards.

"You fucking disgusting animal! You and your whole family!" Gina seethes. She's not screaming, likely because she doesn't want the neighbors to hear. If we were inside, my ears would also be ringing by now.

"Listen to me—"

"No, I will not do a motherfucking thing for you," she interrupts. "What did you and your sleazy family do to my child?"

"Nothing!" I say, trying to get words in before she interrupts me again. "Did Sasha look like she wasn't willing?"

That was the wrong thing to say, but I only realize that after the words leave my mouth.

"Pig!" she hisses, her voice so low she sounds demonic. "When did you touch her? When? How old was she, you monster?"

"No! Wait, stop. I never ever touched her when she was a kid," I say. It's true. I won't say how I imagined I was fucking Sasha the last year or so of my marriage to Gina. I have a feeling that would earn me a ticket to prison. But I am not lying. I never once touched

Sasha until that night when she was eighteen and I walked in on her with a toy between her legs.

"Liar!"

"I am not lying."

"And what about *them*?"

I sigh. "My father and brother also never touched her until she was eighteen and our marriage — you and I —was long over."

"So you waited for her to be of age? And that's supposed to make it better?"

I can't tell her how Tony got with Sasha, that would open a new can of worms that he used to be the Northside Rapist, even though he never technically raped anyone. And she is also not too far off the mark. Without realizing, we did wait until Sasha was eighteen.

Gina is right. I am a pig.

"I am going to the police with these, let them look into this," she threatens.

"They won't. Sasha is in her twenties, and nothing happened while she was underage. The cops may hate the Santinis, but they won't take your case either," I remind my ex.

"The press will take it."

That is what I am afraid of. I need to stop her from doing this, from ruining everything my family built since my father came to this country.

"And what of you? The kids? Maggie and Caleb will grow up being the ones whose dad fucked their half-sister in a funeral home, on top of a casket. Is that what you want for them?"

If looks could kill, my three loves would be fucking on my casket next.

"You will never see the children again. And when I get my hands on Sasha, I will get it out of her, how you three brainwashed and manipulated her!" With that, she slams the door in my face. The last thing I see is Maggie's shocked expression as she enters the foyer behind her mother.

Fuck. How much did she hear? Enough, I suppose, and I know I need to get the Hell out of here. I don't want to fight, especially about this, in front of her.

When I get back home, it's late enough where everyone should be sleeping, but Tony and Dad are awake in the sitting room, both of them looking grim.

"You won the bet," I say as I walk into the room. "It was only by pleading to Gina's love for our other children that she didn't get the cops to investigate all of us — me in particular — for child abuse. Or go to the press."

Dad observes my face and says, "Your cheek seemed to not be immune to her wrath."

"Still red, huh?" I rub it; the skin is warm.

"Hell of a right hook," Tony comments. "And best believe I am not letting you forget about the bet."

"What do we do next?" I ask them. Usually, I am the idea man, but right now I feel so defeated, so dirty, so guilty. I never felt this way unless you count the time I saw Tony fucking Sasha on camera. And that wasn't even a full blown guilt trip.

"Tonight, there is nothing to do," Dad says. "We rest. And we plan tomorrow. There are already people claiming it is that AI bullshit."

"But AI checkers will prove it's real," Tony comments.

He holds a hand up, silencing us both. "I repeat: we cannot do anything without proper rest. Sasha was a mess this afternoon, and she took something to sleep once we got home. With Gina knowing this is true, she may confront Sasha as well. Right now, protecting our piccolina is our top priority."

I nod slowly. As usual, he's right. Sasha first, then we go full steam ahead to protect ourselves and our company. And find out who the fuck was following us.

"I'm gonna go see Sasha," I say. "Is she in her room?" We all have separate rooms, plus the main bedroom, where we usually sleep together.

They nod, so I head upstairs and open the door.

I remember when Sasha moved in with us, the year she began university. Then, her room had boy bands and pink bunnies. Today, there are darker tones, but the gigantic pink rabbit still guards the corner of her room.

Even with our corruption, even with all she's been through, she has that little speck of innocence left in her.

I undo my tie and step over to the bed; if she took something, I expect her to be peacefully sleeping. My plan is to get in bed and hold her a bit.

Until I see her struggling. She's not making noise at the moment, but her body is twitching, and she's fighting against her blankets. A thin sheen of sweat covers her pale forehead.

"Sasha," I whisper, not wanting to startle her. "Little girl, wake up."

All my voice does is make her start to cry and whimper. "Don't." She doesn't usually talk in her sleep. This must be from the medication she took. "Stop, don't hurt her!"

My heart breaks for her; despite it being years ago, she still has nightmares about her best friend from school, Tessa. The summer after graduation, Sasha's insane ex kidnapped both girls. He killed Tessa in front of Sasha, then proceeded to assault her and sell her body to someone else.

Sasha wound up killing him, but it's clear the trauma still lingers somewhere in her mind.

I climb onto the other side of the bed, trying to be gentle and not startle her.

"Get away from me!" In her nightmares, she must be screaming. In reality, it sounds like a muffled drunk slur.

I wrap my arms around her, pulling her to me even as she protests.

"Shh, baby. It's okay. I won't hurt you. Ever."

Still, she struggles, and I hate myself even more as I get hard feeling her wiggle against me, trying to escape.

Maybe I am as bad as Gina said.

"Sasha."

She reacts to her name, but still in the same fearful way, trying to escape. I can't let her stay like this.

This is the last time she's allowed to take anything to sleep, I vow as I follow her movements, laying her out flat on her back. She tries to whack at me, and I know for a fact I don't need to be slapped twice in one day, even if I deserved the first one. I grab both her hands in one of mine, pinning them above her head.

"Be good," I scold, but she whimpers in response.

I have to change whatever nightmare she's having, since I can't wake her. I've heard of being able to help people get into a state of lucid dreaming.

And I can think of one way to induce it.

If I already feel like shit about myself, might as well keep going. In for a penny and all that bullshit.

Sasha sleeps without panties. It's one of the rules we have for her. While she's ours, we get the easiest access possible.

Holding her hands in one of mine still, I let the other trail down her body, over each breast, nipples poking out from under the silk nightie, and she twists her waist, trying to get away.

Reaching the hem, I push it up to her waist, revealing her perfect, soaking wet slit. I want to taste her, but if I let go of her hands, she could hurt one or both of us, so I table that for the future.

I brush her wetness, inserting my hand between her thighs and making her part her legs.

"No..."

I shush her again as I undo my pants, setting my painfully hard cock free. Using my whole body, I lean over her, pinning her down. Her movements drive me insane, every little attempt to escape igniting the flame between us.

"Hold still and let Daddy take care of you," I say, beginning to enter her hot pussy. She's not fully relaxed, and she's tighter than normal because of it.

She cries out when I'm completely inside her, and I hold myself there for a moment. I can't help her get out of her nightmare if I climax in a couple of thrusts. When I begin to move, she feels like Heaven.

Mine. All mine. I share her with my brother and father because I love them too, and I know Sasha does. But here, in this moment, my stepdaughter is my possession.

"Relax and let Daddy fuck you, baby girl," I rasp in her ear, kissing her face, her neck, as I slowly thrust in and out. "You're always safe with me. I love you."

She still cries, and I keep talking her through it, trying to change what goes on in her mind.

"I've got you. No one else can have you, baby. No one else is here. Just me, you, and your sweet little cunt taking my cock like a pro. Relax." She's still tense but no longer fighting me. "Good girl. Now be good for Daddy and come with me. Show me you're mine."

Her whimpers are different this time, higher.

With my free hand, I find her swollen clit and rub; I won't last much longer and I want her to fall off this cliff with me.

She moves her head and cries out in a soft, dreamlike voice. "Daddy..." Her body spasms as she comes around me. "Daddy, please..."

Finally!

That word, her breathy voice, that's all it takes to finally be my undoing and I come deep inside of her filling her up, feeling some of it leak out around me, down her slick thighs.

Still inside her, I let her hands go and she immediately reaches for me, pulling me to her side. I move so she can lay on my chest, not letting my cock escape her warmth.

"Love you," she whispers, tucking herself into my chest like a doll.

She's calm now; for the moment, all is as it should be.

I hold her close, vowing that I will do everything I can to protect this sweet little girl.

Chapter Seven

Sasha

WAKE UP ensconced in warmth, feeling a sense of fullness inside of me.

Daddy. He's still fast asleep, and I see a couple of small cuts on his cheek, too high to be from shaving. Did someone hurt him? I snuggle closer, comforted by his presence, his embrace, and his cock still inside of me. I know we need to wake up and start our day, figure out what to do about those pictures before they're leaked to local media.

In this day and age, we will be all over social media worldwide. Hell, someone might write a taboo novel about us.

I don't want that. I just want to live my life and love my men in peace. Why is that such a Herculean task? First I was stalked and nearly sex trafficked by my crazy ex, who also killed my best friend. Then my estranged father shows up, kills some of our employees, and tries to kidnap me.

When is it enough?

"Little girl," Daddy mutters, his sleepy voice gravelly.

"Five more minutes," I protest.

He moves but doesn't let me go. "Are you okay? You had nightmares last night."

"Is that why your dick is eight inches deep?" I ask with a smile. "I don't remember dreaming or anything."

He makes a noise in his throat. "I had to get you to calm down somehow."

"I know I said I wanted you guys to drug me and fuck me, but I want to be awake for it," I remind him.

He chuckles, though his smile doesn't meet his eyes. His hand comes down sharp on my ass and I squeal. "Cute. Now come on, let's get ready for the day."

"Do we have to? Can't we go to the main bedroom and stay and cuddle and come all day?" I turn my best doll eyes on him, but those never worked. He always saw right through me when I was a kid.

Daddy sighs. "Not when we might have to go on the run, because while what we do with you isn't illegal, what happens between us three men *is*."

Shit. I forgot it's actually illegal, not just immoral.

Fine.

Gently, I pull myself up, letting his cock slip out of me, leaving me feeling empty. I need to do this more often. It's better than a teddy bear.

Once I am showered and dressed, I get to the living room, where Daddy, Nonno, and Uncle Tony now sit, and Uncle Tony's laptop is up on the TV screen, showing the photos in all their debauched glory.

When this is all over, I need to appreciate how hot we all are.

I grab coffee and a banana and sit down with them. "Have they contacted us further?"

Nonno shakes his head.

"They said we had twenty-four hours for you to give them the five million. That time is up … right about now," Uncle Tony says.

My heart leaps into my throat. "So they're going to the press?"

Daddy slowly shakes his head. "I don't think they will. I think they'll try something else first to get the money out of you."

"The money I don't even have! How did they even know who my grandmother was, follow me to the funeral, and figure out how to do all this? I didn't *plan* on fucking on top of a casket!"

"It narrows down the suspects," Nonno says. "It has to be someone who was at the funeral home and got lucky. Also someone who clearly knew only those inheriting something would be in attendance."

A thought hits me and I shudder. "You don't think Julie Kang…"

Uncle Tony shakes his head. "Between her family and the one she married into, this would be petty cash to them. But let me get a message to them and see who in the family they can perhaps give us insight on." He picks up his phone and I go sit in Nonno's lap after I put my coffee mug in the sink and the banana peel in the compost bin.

Nonno puts his arms around my waist and says, "We do have another option that will at least not ruin your future, piccolina."

I turn and face him, twisting in his grip. "If you're daring to suggest—"

"I thought about it too, yesterday," Daddy cuts in, and I swivel to face him this time. "I went to visit your mother, and they did send the pictures to her. I think Maggie might know as well. We can tell the press we brainwashed you, and you can go on and have a future not tainted. That way, they have nothing to hold over you, and we can handle whatever comes our way."

I leap up to stand, turning and looking each man in the eye, stopping on Uncle Tony.

"Do *you* have anything to add to this conversation?" I challenge.

He stands up, towering over me, and I don't back down.

"My brother and father have always had soft hearts. I didn't inherit that little abnormality. So what I have to say is I will not let you go, even if you wanted me to. You belong to me — to us — and no one will ever force me to lie and say this was all some big plan to take and trap you. Though I wouldn't have objected if that was what we had to do." Uncle Tony puts his hand on my chin and jerks it upward, forcing me to look at him.

"Do you understand, tesoro? You belong to us. And once their temporary insanity subsides, they will agree that we will never give you up."

I swallow hard and nod, taken in by his intense gaze, as if he'd lock me up if I tried to get away.

Honestly, the thought isn't unappealing.

Moving away from him, I walk over to stand between the two chairs Daddy and Nonno sit in.

"I'm not usually one to say this, but you both need to listen to Uncle Tony."

"Hey!" he weakly protests from behind me.

Ignoring him, I go on, "How dare you try to deny you've always wanted me, and how much I love you? How dare you think I'd agree to ever lose you? I may be yours, but that goes both ways. You're mine — all three of you. And I will go to Hell itself and back before I let you go."

"We just want you safe," Nonno says, voice softer than I have ever heard it.

"I know," I reply. "But what I want is to be with you, even if we all have to run off and hide on some deserted island. Even if I lose my career, you're my life. And I can't bear to lose that."

Daddy holds my hand and says, "I promised I'd always be there for you and protect you. I don't want to be the reason you're ruined."

"You're too precious to us," Nonno adds.

"And you're precious to me. All three of you," I say, looking around at them all. "And whether or not you want to hear this, you made me this way. Now you get to deal with me for the rest of our lives. Whether you like it or not."

Daddy shakes his head, giving my hand a squeeze. "My stubborn girl. If that's what you want, then we will deal with it and all the fallout."

"And there will be limited fallout if we can figure out what to do to stop these guys short of actually negotiating with them," Uncle Tony adds.

"The thought of paying them off with double is tempting, but they may get greedy and try for even more," Nonno comments.

I pause. "Meet with them to do a money handoff and kill them?"

Daddy sighs. "If only it were that easy. Too many risks to do that."

My phone beeps, and I let go of Daddy's hand to see who is texting, hoping it's a client who is regretful about leaving our firm.

It's Maggie.

"We really need to talk about Dad coming to the house last night."

I lean my head back and let out a frustrated groan. This is not a conversation I want to have. Nor do I think I even have time.

"You should talk to her," Daddy says. "She might take it better from you than from me."

"Sure, because me saying, 'Hey, little half-sister, I'm dating your dad, who was my stepdad, and married to our mother,' is totally fine." I can't help but roll my eyes.

"She has a point," Uncle Tony says.

"Fuck off," Daddy replies, and Nonno smiles at his boys. They may be in their late forties, but they're still his boys at heart.

Daddy stands up and goes for his laptop, which sits idling on the coffee table. "If you go, one thing needs to happen first. You meet with her somewhere we can watch you."

"Watch me?"

He nods, clicks something, and shows me the laptop screen. He has access to CCTV footage I am sure is illegal. It's a small park near Mom's house.

"We're not letting you get taken again," he continues. "This way, if there is trouble, we will find you easily and be able to end it all."

I gnaw at my lip while anxiety bubbles in my chest. "You think they're watching me?"

"We don't know how they knew where you'd be two days ago, so it's a natural assumption," Nonno explains. "But you also can't hide away in this house. Whatever their end game is, we have to ensure they don't ruin your life, or ours. And that begins by acting as if we are not afraid."

I recall something Daddy told me once before my first mock debate in middle school.

"Spit in the face of fear and walk like you own this place."

All right, then.

"I'll meet with Maggie, and hopefully by the end of that you guys will have information or a way to proceed."

"And hopefully the pictures aren't leaked," Daddy says.

In turn, each man kisses me goodbye, with Daddy making sure I have the GPS turned on my phone. Which I always do. Ever since Trevor lured me into that basement from Hell, they have insisted I keep it on all devices I own.

Overprotective? Maybe. But it's easy for me to understand why after what they walked in on. I'm clearly still traumatized from it all. Likely, so are they.

"But you guys still have clients to see," I realize. "Not everyone quit on us after the pictures were sent out."

Nonno impatiently waves me away. "This is worth missing a day of work. Now let's get going. The longer you wait, the more nervous *I'm* going to be."

I nod and kiss each man before I leave.

Just in case anything happens and it's my last chance.

The drive to the park is too short; I don't know what to say to my sister. I guess maybe it will come to me after I get a glimpse of her feelings on all of this. One thing is certain, I won't lie to her. If she's confused about anything, I will tell the whole truth, damning as it is.

She sits on one of the few flat-topped rocks we always used as tables when we were kids, frowning at her phone. Her eyes are narrowed at it, as if she's frustrated or confused by it or something on the screen.

"Hey. Something wrong?" I ask, making sure I don't startle her.

"Oh. Hi. Um, I went to send a text and I have no signal," she says. "Isn't that weird? We're right by our house, we should even be able to pick up Mom's wifi still."

It is weird. Too weird.

I pull out my phone and check. No signal.

Wait. What if that means the signal on the CCTV cameras is jammed too? I know it's possible, as we studied signal jammers and what they can do for class when I was in law school.

"Shit. Maggie, come with me, hurry," I say, grabbing her hand and pulling her up.

"What? Sasha, what's happening?" I drag her towards the parking lot, and then see something that makes me feel like I'm in a bad network crime show: a white van, blocking our path.

"Fuck!" I turn Maggie around so we can run, but it's too late; they're faster.

Before we know it, we're zip tied and tossed into the dark, bare, musky van.

Maggie yells, but I know screaming won't help. Even if people did hear us, it would be difficult in such a big city to even narrow our van down to call the cops. I bet the license plates are fake too.

"Maggie, save your strength," I lightly scold her.

"Does this have to do with the pictures Mom was sent?" she asks.

I sigh. "Likely. And I'm so sorry; you shouldn't be dragged into this. I was probably being followed and didn't fucking notice because I'm too stressed."

She takes a breath, her face ashen even in this murky light back here. "Why? Why is this happening?"

"Grandma's inheritance. They want it. And they know I got the biggest amount, or so it seems they know, anyway," I reply. "I'm sorry they grabbed you too. I will do my best to negotiate for them to let you go once we get to wherever they're taking us."

"How the Hell are you so calm?" she asks. "I'm ready to have a literal heart attack!"

I sigh. "You have no idea the shit I have been through," I admit. "And I'd rather you never know."

I swallow hard, remembering Trevor kidnapping me, using my friend to do it. And when she was of no use, he snapped her neck right before my eyes. I can still hear the sound it made, as well as her body dropping to the basement floor.

I won't let Maggie be hurt because of me.

No one will be hurt because of me. I promise myself that.

"When they stop, as long as we aren't in immediate mortal danger, cooperate with them until I can get them to let you go," I tell her.

"But what about you?"

"Forget me," I snap. "First, get you to safety. Then I can worry about myself."

As I finish speaking, the van stops, then moves again. The rumble of a garage door opening and closing is barely discernible. I can't even gauge how far we drove. Twenty minutes? Not even?

The van doors open and two men in black sweaters and jeans, like a uniform, appear. They're nondescript as can be; you wouldn't be able to pick them out of a crowd. From my line of work, they're the perfect lackeys. So who is the mastermind?

"Scoot forward and let's go," one says. He has a very typical Chicago accent, North Side.

I nudge Maggie, and she gets out first, and I follow. The men grab us by the arms and slam the van door shut.

"Look, it's me you want," I say. "Maggie has nothing to do with any of this, so please let—"

I hear the slap before I feel it, and rage bubbles in my chest. If my hands were free, this fucker would understand

I am not the woman he wants to mess with.

"Shut up; a pretty young girl is always worth something," the second man says, also in a basic Chicago accent, drawing out his "a".

Maggie whimpers and I try to smile to show her I'm okay. I don't think I succeed though.

The men begin to pat us down, but they don't try anything; instead, they take our phones. Well ... there goes my hope I could get through the signal jammer somehow. I'm positive they have one here, too.

We're led into what looks like a nice house; these sort of brownstones are closer to Wrigleyville or downtown. Unless you inherited it, they cost a pretty penny. So I am guessing inheritance, because no way would I be extorted for five million dollars when these houses cost over a million.

I try to glean something of the layout, but I don't get anything useful.

They lead us to a door and down a flight of dimly lit stairs into a large concrete basement. No windows. No light except one long fluorescent bulb on the ceiling. No way to call for help.

"Now, listen well. We are going to cut the ties off," the first man says. "If either of you try anything, the knife I use will suddenly find its way to your throats. Are we understood?"

I nod, gritting my teeth. I am good at self defense, but I have no idea if they're better. If I try anything, I could get Maggie killed.

So I obey like a good little sheep.

Our hands are free and the men walk away silently.

"What the Hell?" I ask. "What do you want?"

They turn, stare, and exit the basement without a word.

"Dammit!" I run a hand through my long, dark hair, wanting to pull it out instead.

"What now?" Maggie asks.

"We wait for them to come back. If they want my money, they need me alive to get it," I say. That's the main reason I'm not panicking yet. They can't kill me. And I am sure they are aware that killing Maggie would not help their cause.

She breathes deeply and leans against the concrete wall. "These past two days are getting progressively worse and worse."

"You're telling me."

I close my eyes, holding onto one more hope.

My men were watching the feed. They surely saw some of what happened, or got suspicious if the cameras were cut. They will find me. I have to believe that. If I can't get us out of here first, they'll come. They always do.

"Since we're stuck..." Maggie trails off, and I glance at her. She's studying her shoes as if they're fascinating. "The pictures..."

Shit. She really wants to do this *now*?

"They didn't force you, did they?" she wonders.

I hold back a laugh. I'm not sure how to explain how it all started to her, because drugging an already drunk girl and fucking her on camera isn't exactly consensual.

Nor is blackmailing me to threaten to tell my mother you caught me masturbating before overpowering me.

Or arranging a meeting for an internship and using that to punish me and the two other men.

"No," I finally say. "I love them." Simple is best, right?

"Like those books? A ... harem?"

I nod. "Yeah, like that."

"And they are... They are together? Isn't that bad?"

Heavily weighing my words, I reply, "Consensual sex between adults is just that."

"Oh. Mom was mad."

"Mom is always mad," I remind her.

She giggles, and I am happy to hear the sound.

"And you? What do you think?" I ask.

"I think ... it's not my business as long as they didn't molest you or force you," Maggie replies. "If you're happy, what else matters?"

I smile at her, opening my mouth to reply, when footsteps echo behind the closed basement door. They're coming.

The door opens and the person thrust inside isn't one of the two men, and when I see him, my whole body feels like a balloon after the air has been let out.

We're fucked.

Chapter Eight

Sasha

"FUCK." MAGGIE LEANS her head against the brick wall as Daddy gets tossed down with us on the filthy concrete floor.

There goes one of our last three hopes for escape.

Immediately he goes to us both, hesitant, his eyes filled with worry. I need him now, but my little sister needs him more, in a different way. She hasn't been traumatized like I have. Hasn't seen this side of humanity. So I let her go to him, and he hugs her tightly, but looks at me over her shoulder.

I give a weak smile. I'm angry, scared, and exhausted, but I'm okay.

Now we need to make sure Maggie stays okay.

"There are no listening devices down here," I tell Daddy. "If we whisper, they can't hear us from the door."

Daddy lets out a sigh of relief. "Good. I let them catch me."

Maggie breaks away from him. "You *what*? Dad, are you out of your mind?"

Daddy smirks. "That is debatable. Are you sure neither of you are hurt?"

Maggie and I both shake our heads.

"They just brought me here and left me. Then Sasha showed up, and same. And now you," Maggie says. "I don't know what they want. This doesn't seem normal, right?"

I shake my head. "It's not normal ... unless they are waiting for something in particular. But I can't imagine what."

"They left a note for us at that park to bring the money," Daddy says. "Clearly they don't realize we are worth much more than five million."

"Clueless and evil. Great combination," I reply. "They also don't realize I don't get that money until I'm married. Add stupid into the mix."

"So they did this because they saw that you're getting a windfall?" Maggie asks me. "Pathetic! Like Dad says, our family is worth much more."

"Better they're clueless," Daddy admits. "Imagine if they got this idea when you were all children?"

I shiver. Trevor abused me since I was fourteen. I could've handled it. But not my little siblings. And I would've gone to Hell and back to rescue them. Just like I am now for Maggie.

"When they come back in, I need you both to do whatever they ask. Don't fight unnecessarily," Daddy says. "They may not do anything, but nothing is worth any of us dying, understood?"

We both nod. I can't imagine what is going through his head, having to protect himself, his daughter, and his stepdaughter-slash-fiancée.

As if his words were a bell to summon them, two men walk into the room. One has a tripod. One has a gun. I'm sure the other is packing too, under that coat.

"Speak of the devils," I mutter.

We don't move as the first man sets up the tripod, aiming it at us.

And then the second one aims the gun, which has a laser light. And it is easy to see it's aimed directly over my heart.

Daddy's jaw tenses but otherwise he doesn't look like he's affected on the outside. Maggie's eyes are wide as saucers. I don't dare to breathe too hard.

"So, Mr. Santini," the man with the gun begins, "evidently you like fucking your children."

"Sasha is not my—"

"Ah ah ah." He wags a finger of his free hand while the other tightens on the gun grip. "You raised her from how old was it again? Five? You can't tell me you don't know how vile what you're doing is? And let's not mention your brother and father?"

"They barely knew me," I argued, lying out my ass.

"Oh, I don't mean them with you," the man says. "I mean how they're all fucking each other as well as you."

Maggie gasps. Apparently Mom has somehow shielded her from that part of the leak. Until now, anyway.

"You didn't know? Poor, stupid child. Your whole family belongs in Hell. And I'll send you there ... as soon as you make us rich."

Daddy holds up his hands in a placating gesture, moving slow so he doesn't startle the man into shooting me.

"If it's money you want, you can have it," he vows. "All of it. Just let us get out of here. The Santinis don't cooperate with the police anyway. You'd all be safe from us and free to go buy an island without extradition."

He's such a clever man, and a quick thinker. I'd be turned on by his mind if I wasn't so preoccupied with not becoming Swiss cheese.

The man chuckles. "I don't think you're aware of it, or more likely you are well aware, what certain black market items can go for."

"You're not going to sell us!" Maggie squeaks, then covers her mouth with both hands.

The man with the camera laughs, the first sound out of him.

"No, I don't have to sell you physically. Already the images and video taken at the funeral home are circulating, earning websites I invested in a lot of money. So I figured ... I should make more. And nothing gets creepy fucks, such as you, Mr. Santini, more turned on than a father raping not one but both his daughters, biological or not. Or better yet, the two in the relationship both ruining the one who isn't. Whores turning on each other is always a hit."

At that, I speak. "You cannot make me hurt my sister. I'd rather die."

"If you're the one who refuses, she's the one who dies." The man shrugs. "Is she better off dead than living, remembering this night over and over? What do you think?"

"I think if I could get close enough to you, I'd make popping my ex's eyeball look like a clip from the Disney Channel."

"Girls." Daddy speaks softly, but the warning is in his voice. His face is so pale, I hope he doesn't make himself sick over this. "You—"

There's a sharp bang, and I feel the bullet whizz by my head, a few inches to my left. It embeds itself in the brick, smoking. My knees feel like jelly but I'm afraid to move to give myself any support.

"Shut. Up. All of you. And do as I say." The gun's laser is back on my chest as if it never moved. "You, little slut, get on your knees next to your sister."

I've never been more grateful to follow an order before. Maggie clings to me like a barnacle.

"I'll make the terms clear. Anyone who balks gets to watch the other two bleed out slowly as they die. And then you get to die."

I glance at Daddy, whose face is drawn and grim. He can't think of a way out of this. Even me, the highest IQ of us all — I'm stumped. Everything ends in tragedy, but only one gives us a chance to live. Maggie is barely holding back tears, her olive skin pale and her eyes watery. They're trying so hard to be strong; I have to be as well.

"Please just go along with it. Rather be alive to hate ourselves later," I whisper, pulling Maggie closer.

She whimpers, and Daddy still looks sick, not taking his eyes from me.

Is he worried about me? That I'll be hurt by this?

"Daddy, you're saving our lives," I say. Maggie nods, head buried in my chest, not seeming to want to look at anyone.

"Camera goes on in five seconds. If you don't begin, he'll be watching as I fuck the bullet holes I put in you two cunts. Understood?" the man barks.

The cameraman begins counting down, and when he says "one", I do the only thing I can think of to start this, since no one else seems to be able to move or think.

I kiss Maggie. I never kissed a girl before, though Trevor always wanted me to. He just had no way to force it. She clings to me like I'm a lifeline, her eyes closed. I look past her to Daddy, whose eyes now register surprise.

Daddy reaches to push Maggie's uniform skirt up and she starts to cry, really cry.

"It's okay," I whisper to her, unsure even if Daddy can hear. "I know you don't want this but—"

"No. It's not that. I just don't want to make him hurt *you* by doing this."

Is she saying she wants...

Oh, fuck it all, our whole family is fucked up, aren't we?

"It won't hurt me, and if you let me help you relax, it won't hurt you, either."

She nods and rests against me.

Daddy has removed her panties and glances at me before unzipping his slacks and taking out a half-hard cock.

A part of me doesn't want him inside anyone else, Uncle Tony included, if I'm being honest. But at the same time, there's a part of me delighted to be a part of this. Some secret, dark part I keep locked up and have locked away since Uncle Tony drugged and fucked me.

I reach down and squeeze Maggie's breasts through her top and she whines when I rub her nipples.

"You're making her so wet for me," Daddy comments.

So he didn't hear her before. Good.

I open Maggie's blouse and push her bra down. She's of a smaller build than me, more like Daddy, while I'm built like Mom. I take a pert nipple in my lips and she gasps. At the same time, her body moves as Daddy pushes inside her in one thrust.

"That's it, Sasha, make her love it. Be my good girl and keep her like that until I'm done," Daddy says, and if I wasn't soaked already, I am now.

My body jolts with each thrust, and Maggie grips me like her life depends on it while I continue to tease her.

Her tears keep falling, and her breathing gets higher and faster; she's going to come.

I hold her still as she crashes over that wave, letting Daddy finish in her without making it any harder for him.

He pulls out of her with his come still leaking, dripping down his shaft, and I don't know why I didn't think he'd do this — he grabs me by the hair and finishes in my mouth, making me taste my sister's sweetness on his cock.

"I'll take care of you later," he promises.

If there is a later.

I take the come still in my mouth and kiss Maggie again, opening her lips with mine. She can taste herself mixed with Daddy as I push his come into her mouth.

The gun laser on my chest flickers, and I remember why the Hell we were doing this in the first place.

It's on Daddy now.

"These two, they will be worth even more with you dead, won't they?" the man with the gun asks.

Life flashes before my eyes as a loud bang hits my ears, and I scream.

Chapter Nine

Sasha

THE WORLD MOVES in slow motion after that bang, and it takes me longer than it should to realize it was a gunshot, but not aimed at Daddy.

The gunman is on the floor, a bullet in his skull. Blood leaks down around his nose like bad special effects, and his eyes are wide, staring eternally at the ceiling.

The door to the basement is open, and I'd recognize those silhouettes anywhere.

Uncle Tony and Nonno.

The cameraman stands there, staring and stammering. He reaches for something but Nonno fires again, this time deliberately hitting the man's knee, sending him to the floor with a cry.

Uncle Tony leaps down the last few stairs and rushes to bind the man, including his mouth.

"Oh, thank God!" I cry, now feeling free enough to get up and hug them both, now that Nonno joined us down here.

"How did you find us?" Maggie asks, hurriedly straightening her clothes.

Daddy shakes his head, grinning. "I had a tracker on me that I dropped outside, before they could search me."

My mouth drops. "You weren't joking: you deliberately got caught?"

His chin jerks to his twin. "His idea."

"Why am I not surprised?" I scrub my face with my hands. "Okay, big shot, what do we do next?" I glance at Uncle Tony, who looks pretty pleased with himself.

He runs his hand along his short beard and says, "We take this fucker with us and interrogate him. After that, the Kangs can dispose of him for us." He glances over at Maggie, eyes worried he said too much.

Nonno walks over to her. "Are you okay?" he asks.

"I will be," she replies. "And don't worry. Whatever I see or hear ... I'm not going to say a word or judge." She gives a shudder as she watches the writhing, angry, bound man on the floor. "I'm just glad to be alive and not shot to death or sold off."

"Speaking of..." Daddy walks past, goes to the camera, and takes out the memory card, pocketing it.

Uncle Tony and Nonno glance at it, but neither say anything.

"All right, let's get Maggie home, then take this fucker on a ride," Uncle Tony says.

As soon as he finishes speaking, a door slams and multiple angry, loud voices can be heard, as well as stomping feet.

"Shit," both twins say at once.

"You didn't happen to bring more guns, did you?" I ask as the footsteps get closer. Three people? More? It's hard to tell. I don't like guns, but I know how to shoot if I have to.

Nonno scowls. "Should have. Didn't want to be weighted down."

"I thought it was just these two," Uncle Tony said. "CCTV footage showed only them for you girls."

The door to the basement opens again, and four men scramble down the stairs, two of them letting off bullets which, thankfully, go wild. They don't look like the other two. While the dead guy and the one tied up have a sort of street gangster vibe, these men in suits seem more like the higher ups, the ones who never have to get their hands dirty.

Scum always answers to people better than them; I should've seen this coming.

"Back up!" one man barks at Uncle Tony and Nonno, who are closest.

Uncle Tony shields me, while Daddy protects Maggie. Not that he should, since he also doesn't have a weapon.

The bound man struggles more, trying to get free.

The man who seems to be in the lead scoffs. "Fucking trash." He then raises his gun and shoots the man twice in the head, ending his life.

Maggie can't help but let out a yelp, either of surprise, fear, or disgust, I don't know.

The four men slowly surround us, and it's clear why Nonno and Uncle Tony are hesitant to shoot. They can hit two men, but that leaves two more who may also be packing, who can kill us just as quickly.

Fuck fuck fuck.

Why do we always get into these messes? Is it too much to just want to hide away and work and fuck my men in peace?

"We should thank you," the man in the lead comments. He looks vaguely familiar, but I have no idea where I could have seen or met him before. At work? Did we defend him at some point?

"Thank us?" I ask.

"You got rid of these two fuckwits for us," he explains. "Imagine thinking you, the Santini heiress, is only worth a mere five million dollars? We just wanted them to get you here, and anyone else we could use." He smirks. "And now there are four of us with weapons, and only two of your men have them. It looks like we can take you and your sister with us. If they want you back, and don't want the press to see those pictures I took, they can pay us whatever they think you're worth."

"*You* took?" Daddy asks. "How did you even know where we would be or what we'd be doing?"

"Your precious Sasha's grandmother was a … patron of my funeral home last week," he explains. "After all, who expects a place to house the dead to be a money laundering scheme? I knew who you all were, all of Chicago does. And I was right to follow you and see what you were up to in that empty room."

Please be stupid and keep talking, I think, hoping we can keep the guns aimed away from us a bit more. I look over at Maggie, who has something in her hand. It's a piece of concrete, which must have went flying when a bullet hit the wall by us.

Don't do anything ridiculous, I think. *This isn't a movie!*

However, I don't listen to myself, as I spot the corpse of the second man near me, hidden behind Uncle Tony and Nonno's combined bulk.

I move.

One of the underlings sees and shoots at me, but it doesn't hit anything vital. Instead, it grazes my cheek, causing blood to course down my face, hot and sticky.

Worth it to get the gun and shoot that man three times in the chest and stomach, sending him flying backwards, crashing into the wall before he falls to the floor.

That was the distraction Uncle Tony and Nonno needed to dispatch one more man, but the fourth one is swift. He grabs me, aiming the gun at my head, but he's not expecting the piece of concrete to connect with the back of his head, courtesy of Maggie.

I get the time I need to turn in his loosened grasp and shoot him as well. It's not immediately fatal, but it will keep him out of our hair as he slowly bleeds out from the gut.

"Little bitch!" the ringleader yells, aiming his gun.

Uncle Tony gets there first, splattering the wall behind the man with blood and brains.

"Don't fucking talk to my fiancée like that, you prick."

Finally, the last man gets to his knees, gun dropped, hands behind his head in surrender. Unlike his boss, he's not stupid. If surrendering will keep him alive, he will lose all dignity and self-respect.

Disgusting.

"How many more of you are there in this little ... do we even call this an organization?" Nonno wonders.

"N-No one. Sir. I mean, it was just us, we're small-time, trying to get money and grow," the man on his knees stammers.

While he talks, Uncle Tony brings me a handkerchief and presses it to my cheek to stop the bleeding. I'm going to need stitches.

"Do we believe him?" Daddy asks.

I nod slowly. "A bigger organization wouldn't be this sloppy."

Maggie raises her eyebrows at me, as if to say she didn't consider three kidnappings and forced sex on camera "sloppy".

"Please. Please let me go. I didn't shoot anyone, I didn't have anything to do with this but follow along!" he begs.

"But you were going to let them take us and keep the money, weren't you?" Maggie snaps, startling all of us.

Daddy puts a calming hand on her shoulder. I should be jealous, but I'm not. I know Uncle Tony, Nonno, and me are all Daddy wants, and my sister needs comfort.

"You heard my granddaughter. Why should we let you go?" Nonno asks.

"Do we kill him too, or turn him in? After all, it's his friends' bullets in all these people," Uncle Tony comments. "Friendly fire, mass murder."

I step forward and kneel in front of the terrified former gangster, whose eyes widen in terror. I must be a sight, smirking at him while soaked in my own blood.

"Turn him in," I say. "The Kangs can get any digital traces of the images wiped once they come get him."

Relief washes over his face. "T-Thank you."

I lean closer, smiling wider even though it hurts. "I hope in prison someone forces your weak bitch ass the same way your deceased colleagues forced the three of us. And I hope someone records your misery. Even I'd be paying to see it."

The relief vanishes from his face as fast as it arrived, and his skin looks ashy. Yeah. He knows what will happen to a stool pigeon in jail. He should've begged for death. At least then maybe I would've considered it.

Standing, Nonno puts a protective arm around my waist. "I am sorry we didn't get here sooner, piccolina."

"It's okay. You still made it. Now let's call the Kangs, get everything removed, and have some fucking peace for once."

"Now that, tesoro, is the best idea you have ever had."

Chapter Ten

Sasha

One year later...

HE SOFT SPRINGTIME sun reflects off the water at Jeju Island, and from my hotel room window, I can see everything set up on the shore. Well, almost everything.

"Hey, it's time," Maggie says softly from the doorway.

I take a breath and stand up, turning to see her smiling at me. It's been a year, and we never talked about what happened when we were trapped in that basement with Daddy. Sometimes she finds it hard to look at me, and I don't know if it's because of the scar on my face as a reminder of that night or the shame that she admitted to being attracted to him. Maybe I should ask, but that little heart-to-heart won't happen today.

I'm kinda busy.

"Scared?" she asks me.

I nod. "Kinda. Ever since last year, we kept such a low profile. Now there's press here."

She waves a hand as if swatting a fly. "You guys managed to convince people that was all fake, and even revealed the kidnappers were forcing you to film more fake content. It was good to lay low, but now it's time to re-emerge into the world. As you are. Not hiding."

She's right. My baby sister shouldn't have more common sense than me.

"I wish Mom was here."

I did send her an invitation, but she hasn't spoken to me or my men since she found out about us. Likely she never will again, and I have to make peace with that.

How ironic her mother shut her out after a man hurt her, yet she shut me out after I found love? What a fucked up cycle. If I get pregnant, I will break that cycle. My kid could be a serial killer, and I am not going to ever cut them out.

I walk to the door, checking to make sure nothing can get on the train of my dress. It was deliberately designed to not drag on the floor, but I'm still paranoid. Okay, I'm vain. But vanity isn't the worst sin I will commit today.

A sole older lady gets on the elevator with us, sees me, and says, "Chukhahapnida!"

"Gamsahapnida," I reply with a smile.

After we exit the hotel, the wedding planner meets up with us, her pink and blonde hair in a perfect, K-pop twist. "Mrs. Santini!" she calls, brash and loud. Probably why she isn't an idol but instead organizes weddings. "You were almost late! Little Miss Santini, the march is about to start."

It's not a wedding march; we chose to have me walk down the aisle to Oasis' "Let There Be Love".

Our guests, precious few of them, and sadly my mother and baby brother not amongst them, turn when the music changes and swells, and I walk under the makeshift awning adorned with purple and white lilies. My men wait for me at the altar overlooking the ocean.

Nonno is dressed the most traditionally, his silver fox hair slicked back and wearing a black penguin-type tuxedo.

Daddy has his brown hair in a similar style, his blue eyes reflecting the ocean behind him. His suit is more modern, and his tie is the only thing that is white.

Uncle Tony's hair is pulled back in a ponytail so the wind doesn't make it obscure his face. He's wearing black silk, except his tie, which is blood red. His waistcoat has a nearly imperceptible snakeskin pattern, which matches his boots.

They're all so perfect, so different, so *mine*. In spirit and in name.

Uncle Tony and I signed a legal marriage certificate back in Chicago, and this is the true ceremony, the handfasting, as it's called.

The money I was owed is now sitting split in my siblings' bank accounts. The family fortune isn't what I inherited from my late grandmother. No, the real family fortune is right here, in front of me.

My husbands watch me with matching expressions of awe and love, and I feel as though I don't deserve such reverence. My steps don't falter, but I swallow hard, not wanting to cry now. Just from seeing them?

And then I realize Nonno and Daddy both have tears in their eyes, and Uncle Tony's also look suspiciously red.

If this was another world, Daddy would be walking me down the aisle to marry someone … well, someone I don't call "Daddy".

I reach them and the officiant, and each man kisses my forehead or face in turn. We stand in an odd semicircle so our guests can see us, and we can see each other and the officiant.

"Handfasting is an age-old symbol of strength and love, of continued commitment and steady devotion. It signifies a willingness and desire to grow alongside one another, facing each new day as a team. Drawing on individual strengths while learning to accept each other's help and support. It communicates the belief that together you will meet challenges you could never meet alone.

"Sasha, Anthony Senior, Anthony Junior, and Eugene Santini, you have come here to become handfasted to one another. To pledge to yourselves and to your family and friends that you will continue to love and support one another, growing stronger together each day. Is this true?"

All three of us agree at once, in a chorus.

"As head of the family, Anthony Senior will recite the vows on behalf of your partners, Sasha."

I am so nervous, I forgot we wrote vows. Fuck, I hope I remember mine.

Nonno clears his throat, and while he speaks, Daddy and Uncle Tony each take one of my hands in one of theirs.

"Our sweet Sasha, the circumstances of how we came into one another's lives were inauspicious at best, criminal at worst. But time and life flowed on, as they are wont to do, and circumstances changed. Lives changed. You grew up into the beautiful young lady we began to court years ago. And while each of us fell for you at different points in time, there is no denying the truth we all knew: you were ours. And we belonged to you.

"Our strong, intelligent, beautiful, brave girl. It was a pleasure watching you grow up. It is a privilege to love the woman you have become. And it is our honor to call ourselves your husbands.

"We vow to love, protect, cherish, and adore you for the rest of our lives, and even beyond. Forever, we are yours."

Dammit, now I am crying, but silently.

Uncle Tony wipes away tears on one side, Daddy on the other.

I clear my throat this time, trying to get my wits about me to speak.

"It feels like time flew by so fast, some of the details are hazy. One moment I was exiting a horrible relationship, and the next I was surrounded by more love than I ever thought I deserved, giving back more love than I thought I was capable of pouring out.

"Falling in love with you three wasn't a choice: it was an inevitability. I couldn't stop it, even when I knew it would be frowned upon. It would be as futile as trying to stop a hurricane. And I didn't want to stop it, and I never will.

"I vow to be the best wife, the best friend, the best partner you will ever need. I vow to always be there for you three, to care for you. I vow to love you with every last breath, with every part of my soul. Because my heart is not enough; I love you with all that I am, and I vow to show you every single day.”

I try to hold it together, I swear. But when Uncle Tony lets a tear slip, that’s it for me and I have to remember to breathe through the soft sobs.

“Baby girl,” Daddy whispers, kissing my head.

“Cry later, piccolina,” Nonno says with a small smile. “We aren’t done here.”

“Yes, sir,” I reply, trying to save my makeup. I’m gonna have to send the brand a thank you basket of muffins; there’s no eyeliner on my hands when I look at them.

The officiant knows we aren’t going to use rings; we will be getting tattoos tomorrow. We already have the artist booked.

The four of us place our hands together, all of them touching, and the officiant begins to wind the rope around our wrists, symbolically binding us together forever.

"I pronounce you handfasted and partners in this life. Thank you for sharing this day with us, and may this bond continue to strengthen the love you already feel for one another."

As we lean in and my men kiss me, the rope loosens and falls from our wrists, as it's supposed to.

Uncle Tony grabs it before it hits the ground.

"You're keeping it as a memento?" The officiant smiles at us.

"We're keeping it for something," Uncle Tony replies, and his smile is practically wolfish.

We have a small reception, catered by one of the best restaurants in Seoul, and a traditional first dance.

My men take their turns with me, one by one, as we dance to Amaranthe's "Unified" inside the hotel ballroom.

It is everything I could have wanted and more.

We toast with limoncello at the end of the night, despite the food being Korean. Can't take the Italian out of the Italians, I suppose.

"Where did you get this?" It's a good quality bottle.

"I brought it just for us," Uncle Tony replies with a wink.

A hotel attendant, at the end of the reception, drives us to the little off-site bungalow we rented. We'll spend a week here for our first honeymoon, then head to Sicily for another week.

As we reach the doorway, Daddy picks me up and sweeps me into his arms. I giggle and lay my head on his chest as my men lead me into the little cabin with a cliffside view of the sea.

I don't really get to see the living room as they walk quickly into the only bedroom. There's no light, but the moon outside is more than bright enough to see by.

They plop me in the middle of the California king-sized bed, and immediately Uncle Tony has my wrists captured in his hand.

"What the—"

He shushes me as he uses the rope from the handfasting to tie my hands to the slatted headboard behind me, leaving me vulnerable and defenseless.

And then the room begins to spin.

That's not supposed to happen, right?

"I think it's hitting her, Tony," Daddy comments.

Nonno glances down at me — or is that up? — and nods. "It appears so. Just in time."

"What?" My voice is shuddery to my ears, distant. Like I'm speaking through water. The parts of my body not tied up are heavy and hard to move, but I can still feel them. My thoughts won't focus fully, instead dancing between curiosity and fear.

"Don't you remember your request for us? Before all Hell broke loose?" Uncle Tony asks me, and his grin is wry, almost feline.

Request? I had a request?

Oh shit.

"I want you guys to roofie me and film yourselves fucking me."

I said that, didn't I?

"Fuck," I manage to slur and the men laugh.

"There are cameras set up all over the room. You will have the best honeymoon souvenir you could have imagined," Daddy says, running his hand under my white dress, up my stocking'd leg, and back down the other one.

He begins to undress me while Uncle Tony and Nonno undress each other in my line of sight. Uncle Tony wraps his hand around Nonno's cock and pumps, getting his father to full hardness.

Meanwhile, Daddy slips my dress completely off and places it somewhere outside my line of sight. He steps back to the edge of the bed and stares at me, clad in panties and sheer white stockings.

"My little girl, all grown up but still as beautiful as the day I first fucked you," he comments. Bending down, he slips my panties off, leaving the stockings on.

"Too bad I want to use her mouth," Uncle Tony comments. "We could have gagged her with those."

"Gagging her with cock is better," Nonno comments. He walks past Daddy, stroking his cock for him as he does, then lets it go and stands at the side of the bed, kneeling down.

He bends over, taking a nipple in his mouth and biting down. I whimper; while my extremities are numb, apparently my wet pussy and hard nipples are just fine.

Uncle Tony comes to my other side, moving so his cock is at my lips. "Kiss the cock that owns you, tesoro," he commands.

I do as he asks, barely able to move my head.

He takes a fistful of hair, which had been stylishly done in a loose updo, in a strong fist and shoves my face down, his cock passing the back of my throat. "That's it, take it all. Choke on it."

Nonno grabs my breasts in both his hands, pulling them outward and inserting his cock between them, now slick with his spit, so he could use them as masturbation tools.

"Every inch of our little bride was made to take cock," he comments. "A walking, talking fucktoy. And all ours."

Fuck, they've dirty talked before. A lot. But it seems like between the cameras, the drugs, and knowing I belong to them legally now has unleashed new sides, and my depraved cunt is literally dripping because of it.

Daddy shoved two thick fingers inside me, shocking me with the sudden stretch, and fucks me mercilessly with them. His thumb presses against my clit and his two fingers hit that spot inside me and I come in a minute or two, soaking his hand as I squirt around him.

Removing his fingers, he gives them to Uncle Tony to lick, which he does as well as he can take Daddy's cock.

"Fucking delicious," Uncle Tony comments. With a grunt, he takes his cock from my mouth and Nonno takes his place, moving slower, making it last longer. Knowing even if I wanted to escape this, I can't. I can't even speak to use a safeword.

"Let me get some of her cunt juice on me," Uncle Tony tells Daddy. "For our wedding gift, I'm going to break her asshole."

I whimper around Nonno's cock, the most sound I can make, and all three men laugh.

"Did you think we'd go easy on you? This is what you asked for, so take it like a good girl and maybe we'll do it again," Nonno promises. "And no, we won't tell you when." He grabs my hair too, holding his cock down my throat, and I have to force myself to breathe through my nose.

Uncle Tony runs his cock along my wetness and all three move me so I am a bit on my side. In an instant, he shoves his cock inside me, and it doesn't hurt as much as it should because of whatever they gave me.

Tomorrow, it will be agony.

But for tonight, my step uncle, my husband, can rape my ass and I won't do a thing about it.

Daddy enters me, finally, blue eyes shining in the half-light.

"Did I ever tell you, my sweet bride, why I finally decided to divorce your mother?" he asks.

"You never even told us," Uncle Tony comments.

"Because it worried me every time I'd come, I'd be picturing your sweet little pussy instead and had to stop myself from making a late night visit one too many times."

At his words, I come. I can't help it.

Lord knows I'm fucked up.

Dad finishes in me, filling me up, and pulls out, his cock still at half-mast, and Nonno replaces him while Uncle Tony steadily brutalizes my ass.

Nonno enters me, nodding to Daddy. "Choke her. I want to see what lasts longer: her lungs or my cock."

Another whimper from me as Daddy does as his dad asks and wraps his hand around my throat, squeezing.

Just as I think I'm about to pass out, Nonno comes with a grunt and syas, "Fuck, she always tightens up just before she passes out."

Uncle Tony comes hard and pops out of my ass. I figure he's done, but no. He's now the third husband inside of me, holding my limp legs up as he pounds away, hitting that sensitive spot over and over at a perfect angle.

Daddy makes me suck his cock, and even Nonno is still hard.

Did they all take something?

I swallow Daddy's hot come , but barely. He massages my throat with his hand to ensure I don't choke, then turns my head to Nonno, who shoots a load into my mouth that I can't do anything with. It will sit in there until I can move again.

My breaths come in pants, and the only sounds now are mine and their breathing, and the wet slaps of Uncle Tony's cock as he pushes Nonno and Daddy's cum back inside me.

Daddy goes down and licks his brother's cock as it moves in and out of me, while Nonno lazily plays with my tits again.

Then Daddy sucks my clit as Uncle Tony thrusts deeper and I shatter a third time, squirting out around him as he fucks me through the orgasm and finally — finally — shoots his second load of the night into me.

I'm so exhausted.

Daddy undoes the rope around my hands, Uncle Tony goes to get something to clean me off with, and Nonno removes the stockings from my legs before all three climb into bed.

I'm still numb, but it's wearing off just a bit in my extremities and mouth.

Thankfully not my ass. Yet.

"Love you," I manage to slur out.

"We love you too, piccolina," Nonno says.

"We always have," Daddy adds.

"And always will. And now we are a proper family," Uncle Tony says.

We are.

The Santinis; finally truly family
in every way that matters.

The End

Author's Note

Lord in Heaven help me. And help all my faithful Sinners who waited so long.

Let me tell a story. This was supposed to be published in 2023. *2023!* When it was ready for upload, Word crashed. Not only myself but many others lost manuscripts, or had files become corrupted. I lost this whole finished manuscript. Not to mention seven (count it: SEVEN!) files for clients that took me over two months to redo.

I had no idea the unfinished file was what remained uploaded after the "final" file was submitted and summarily rejected.

Thank God I had notes, both for myself and my clients.

However, between losing that work and having other deadlines and projects, it was nearly impossible for me to properly sit down and work on this book again. Add to that the crushing blow to the psyche it is to lose 22k words when my output is not nearly as fast as most of my contemporaries'.

I knew many, many people were waiting for the finale of the Santini Family, and I also felt the pressure to make the rewrite as good as (or better than) the original manuscript that was lost.

Personally, I think this version is better. I added a new twist regarding Maggie, and the last chapter, to me, is one of my favorite things I have ever written.

I want to thank each and every one of you for waiting for me, for this book, for Sasha and her men. I hope they were worth it. I hope you loved the ending, and maybe, just maybe, you will see them again in 2025... (No, there isn't a fourth book, but there's something cooking over in the Sinclair kitchen.)

And please stick around! I have a lot coming in the latter half of 2024, and in 2025 as well! I plan on getting more debauched, more blasphemous, and filthier than ever! More RH, some monster cocks, and very bad things going down in church confessionals are the tip of the iceberg.

I hope you will join me for these wild rides.

All my twisted love to each and every one of you, my Sinners!

Serena ♥

About the Author

S.L. Sinclair is a dark romance and taboo author fascinated with human sexuality, murder, and psychology. *Beyond Her Duties* was her first release, which made her an international bestseller. Followed by the surprise smash hit *The Family Firm*, cementing her in the dark and taboo genres of romance.

They're part of the LGBT+ community as bisexual and nonbinary and uses she/they pronouns.

When not writing, she's watching horror movies and has her nose buried in whatever book is closest. Sometimes she actually goes outside.

You can find them on Facebook, Twitter, Goodreads, BookBub, and Instagram.